Snowy Sports

Ready, Set, Play!

Per-Henrik Gürth

Kids Can Press

Ready for lots of winter fun?
Dress warmly and let's go play!
long johns

Ice skating
Take a twirl on the ice.
mittens

Sledge hockey
Scoot, shoot and score!
earmuffs

Hockey
Pass the puck — who's open?
hockey stick

Speed skating
Dash ahead and lean into the corner.
skates

Curling
Yay! Good throw!
jacket

Bobsleigh
Ready? Set? GO!
helmet

Skeleton

Rocket along the curve — zoom!

Luge
Slip and slide down the track.
sled

Downhill skiing
Zippity-zip down the snowy hill.
hat

Ski jumping
Soar high above the cheering crowd.
skis

Freestyle skiing
Twist and flip through the air!
ski poles

Snowboarding

Ride the half-pipe — do an ollie!

Cross-country skiing
Glide along the trail, swish-swish.
scarf

What a day! Time to warm up by the fire. Hot chocolate for everyone!
boots

For Fredrik and William

Kids Can Press acknowledges the financial support of the Government of Ontario, through the Ontario Media Development Corporation's Ontario Book Initiative; the Ontario Arts Council; the Canada Council for the Arts; and the Government of Canada, through the BPIDP, for our publishing activity.

Published in Canada by
Kids Can Press Ltd.
29 Birch Avenue
Toronto, ON M4V 1E2

Published in the U.S. by
Kids Can Press Ltd.
2250 Military Road
Tonawanda, NY 14150

www.kidscanpress.com

The artwork in this book was created in Adobe Illustrator.
The text is set in Providence-Sans Bold and Good Dog Plain.

Written and edited by Yvette Ghione
Designed by Karen Birkemoe and Kathleen Gray
Printed and bound in China

This book is smyth sewn casebound.

CM 09 0 9 8 7 6 5 4 3 2 1

Library and Archives Canada Cataloguing in Publication

Gürth, Per-Henrik
Snowy sports: ready, set, play! / by Per-Henrik Gürth ; [written by Yvette Ghione].

ISBN 978-1-55337-367-4

I. Ghione, Yvette II. Title.

PS8613.H56 S63 2009 jC813'.6 C2008-907929-9

Kids Can Press is a Corus™ Entertainment company